AND OTHER CREEPY TALES

Matchstick Man

and other creepy tales

Ruth Morgan

Gomer

To all at Fairfield School

Published in 2009 by Pont Books, an imprint of
Gomer Press, Llandysul, Ceredigion SA44 4JL
Reprinted: 2018

ISBN 978 1 84851 053 1

A CIP record for this title is available from the British Library.

This book is published with the financial support of the
Welsh Books Council.

Printed and bound in Wales at
Gomer Press, Llandysul, Ceredigion SA44 4JL

Matchstick Man

Griff lived along the winding road which led out of town. It was a perfectly normal road, with a mixture of houses and bungalows, and the occasional patch of rough ground as it got closer to the country. But just before the last street light stood a strange old house. I suppose it was standing, just about. There'd been a fire there years and years before and it was really just a shell. Griff hardly ever had a reason to walk past it. But whenever he did, something drew him to stop and stare a few moments, holding onto the forbidding front gates which were secured with rusty chains and a padlock.

The house was very big and the strangest thing about it was the position of the front door. It was halfway up the building. Griff always imagined some city business-man leaving for work one morning with a rolled-up newspaper under his arm, calling 'see you tonight, darling!' over his shoulder as he opened the door, his expression turning to one of horror as he plunged the fifteen feet or so down into the garden. Of course, there must have been a staircase leading up to the door at one time, perhaps one of those fancy iron or marble affairs. The salvage men must have come and taken it after the fire.

Griff didn't give the old house a great deal of thought until he had to do a digital photography project for school. This meant that each pupil in turn had a chance to borrow a high-spec camera in order to photograph something of interest in the local area. After tea one evening, Griff persuaded his sister, Catrin, to take a walk up the road with him.

'Ugh,' said Cat, when she realised what she'd agreed to. 'What do you want to take a picture of that old dump for?'

'I like it,' said Griff. 'It's got atmosphere.'

'Well, let's get home before dark, that's all.' It was early November and the nights were drawing in.

'Why?'

'I just don't like it. Tŷ Lludw. Ash House. Even the name makes me nervous.'

'It won't take long,' said Griff.

'Better not. You know what they say happened, don't you?' Cat's voice dropped to a whisper. 'Someone burnt it down on purpose; but the bloke who did it didn't manage to get out in time.'

'Ugh!' said Griff. 'You mean . . . ?'

Cat nodded and clutched at her throat to make the point.

They reached the gates and Cat leant against one of the ivy-smothered gateposts as Griff took a few shots of the house. After the last, he stared at the house with a new, grim respect. What a horrible story! It wasn't a businessman he imagined coming out of the door now, but a desperate-looking man holding a box of matches. What if the collapsing staircase had trapped him?

'Come on, let's get home,' pleaded Cat. 'I can't stand it here much longer.'

The next day at school, Griff and his classmates were up in the IT suite, loading the photos they'd taken onto the computers and then printing them out. Griff was working on the same machine as his mate Anthony, and of course he couldn't resist telling his friend the gruesome story of Tŷ Lludw.

Anthony's pictures of the local park were really dull, as he admitted himself. By contrast, Griff's photo was stunningly atmospheric: the last rays of the setting sun glinting off the broken windowpanes, scrubby bushes growing out of crevices high up in the walls and the whole house framed by those enormous rusty gates in the foreground. It was only after Griff had printed off his photo that he noticed what his so-called 'mate' had done.

Back at the computer, Anthony was laughing uncontrollably, his face buried in his arms. Griff rushed back and took another look at the monitor.

'You div! You've ruined it!' Griff pushed Anthony, sending him spinning round on his chair. Somehow, before Griff had pressed 'print', Anthony had managed to draw on top of the image. Right in the foreground stood a 'stick man' in a black hat, all wiggly and hurriedly drawn, holding what was obviously supposed to be a lighted match. The stick man had a face like a little kid might have drawn, except his V-shaped eyebrows gave him an evil look.

'He's not a stick man. He's a "matchstick man", geddit?' squealed Anthony.

'I'm gonna kill you!' Griff was trying hard not to laugh himself, though.

'You can click *undo*. Go on, quick, print it out again,' Anthony urged but the lesson was over; it was the end of the day and everyone was packing up to go home. At least the teacher hadn't seen what had happened, luckily for Anthony. The whole school was on economy red alert over the misuse of printer paper and ink. On their way out, Griff made Anthony promise that they'd both sneak up to the IT suite at breaktime the following morning to print the photo out properly.

That evening, Griff was trying to find something in his school bag when he came across the picture, all scrunched up under his homework. There was no sense in keeping it; he might as well throw the stupid thing away. Even so, Griff smoothed it out to take another look. After staring for some time, he tilted the lampshade up to see if he was imagining things. The matchstick man was in a different place from earlier. Instead of standing at the front of the picture, he was now halfway across the garden, heading for the house. The figure was also facing away from the viewer, its face not visible any more, but it was still holding onto the lighted match.

Griff scowled. Typical of Anthony, he always kept jokes going way past the point of being funny. Somehow, he had changed the original picture yet again and printed out this second version. As they'd been packing up their things, Anthony must have switched this one for the original printout. Amazing that he'd actually been smart enough to pull off such a stunt without Griff knowing.

Only Anthony denied it. The next morning at school, Griff collared his mate and accused him of switching the prints. Anthony denied it all, even when Griff showed him the new picture. He insisted it was Griff who must have changed the matchstick man's position on his own computer at home. The argument went past the point either boy thought was funny and the result was that when Griff sneaked up to the IT suite at breaktime, he was on his own.

The picture was scrunched up worse than ever following the argument and Griff knew the bin was the best place for it but he just had to take a last look before throwing it away. One last look, no harm in that, was there? His heart seemed to be telling him otherwise, beating faster as he drew the picture slowly from his bag. He didn't want to put the main lights on in case he drew attention to himself, so he went over to the window and pulled the cord to angle the vertical blinds open. Then he placed the paper on the desk next to the window and slowly, hesitantly, smoothed out the creases.

His eyes travelled over the image and his heartbeat doubled, trebled in speed the instant he saw the change. Matchstick Man had arrived at the house but was floating in mid air. *He was climbing a staircase which wasn't there any more.* The image swam before Griff's eyes as his mouth went dry and his legs felt as though they were about to give way.

He'd kept his bag near him all morning. Anthony hadn't had any chance to switch the print again. What was happening?

Griff backed away, groping for the door, unable to take his eyes off the image.

Somehow, Anthony was still to blame. If he hadn't drawn Matchstick Man in the first place, none of this would be happening. Griff was going to run down and fetch Anthony from the yard. He was going to make him see what he'd done.

Five minutes later, Anthony was standing next to Griff in the IT suite and both boys were examining the print, which still lay on the desk. 'I think you're going crazy,' said Anthony. He turned to Griff with a baffled expression. 'You've just printed your photo out again, haven't you? Properly this time.'

Griff shook his head and stared incredulously at the photo. There was no sign of Matchstick Man in front of Tŷ Lludw.

'No.' Griff was nearly in tears. 'Look, the front door's open. It wasn't open when I first took the picture, don't you remember? He's inside! Matchstick Man's gone inside!'

'Matchstick Man's just a stupid drawing,' said Anthony. 'I know you were annoyed that I spoiled your first print but there's no need to go this far. It's over, OK? Just put that in your bag and let's get out before someone catches us.' He held out the photograph for Griff to take.

Now it was Griff's turn to stare at Anthony as though he were mad. 'I don't want it!' he cried, backing towards the door.

The sirens blared past Griff's house just as it was growing dark.

'Fire engines,' said Cat. 'Wonder where they're off to?'

Griff knew at once. And the following morning, he and his family took a walk up the road, where other locals had gathered to see Tŷ Lludw or rather what was left of it. Literally a house of ashes now.

The firemen had had to smash the gates open so now there was an unobstructed view of the smouldering wreckage lying all over the ground, not a wall left standing. No one could understand how it had happened although vandals were the likeliest bet.

When Griff got back home, there was a message on the answerphone.

'Hi. It's Anthony. Ring me back as soon as you can, yeah? It's that picture, the one you wouldn't have back. I don't know why; I took it home. The thing is, I know it's going to sound crazy but . . . but the picture's changed again. The house has gone, Griff, but it's worse than that . . . He's back. You know who I mean. I'm looking at him now. He hasn't got the match any more but he's looking this way!

'Griff, it's like he's looking at me . . .'

Hide and Seek

What do you think it would be like to stay the night in a museum?

I know someone who did: it was me. I'll never forget that night or the strange story I have to tell about it. Last Christmas, just before we broke up for the holidays, our class got the chance to take part in a story sleepover, right slap bang in the middle of the Great Hall in the National Museum in Cardiff. You know what it's like by day, that massive marble hall downstairs? Well, on a cold winter's night with all the lights off, except the tiny white lights of the Christmas tree, it feels even bigger.

We'd had a great laugh, telling each other ghost stories earlier that evening, huddled round in our sleeping bags, sipping hot chocolate with marshmallows melting on top like sweet, sticky snow. It was easy being brave then. It was when darkness fell and I found myself lying in the worst place, right at the edge of the group, that I felt the first prickle of fear. My pocket torch was worse than useless: its feeble beam barely reached the nearest pillar. The empty floor lay to one side of me, racing away into the dark. I was determined I wasn't going to turn my back on it, not for a moment.

'Mr Meredith, is the museum haunted?' whispered a voice close by. I knew it was my mate Carly, who'd been trying to freak me out all evening by sticking her torch under her chin.

'Shush!' I nudged her.

'I've never heard of there being any ghosts here *as such*,' our teacher replied. I could just make out his profile in the dark, a nose and moustache sandwiched between his Wales hat and scarf. 'But I've often wondered about those old dinosaurs next door. Who thinks they might wake up at night and go for a prowl? Perhaps they go upstairs to study the paintings.'

I wished he hadn't made that joke. Immediately in my mind we were no longer in the Great Hall, the lot of us, but lying at the bottom of a vast cave carved into the side of a Welsh mountain. When my hand slid from my sleeping bag onto the marble floor, it rested on a prehistoric cold. Far above in the shadows of the great round dome, pterodactyls were roosting, their leathery wings folded up like umbrellas and, any minute now, the hungry dinosaurs would come galumphing in. There we lay like snacks on a tray. Why on earth hadn't we pitched our beds next to a wall instead of lying so exposed? Oh yes, that's right: Mr Meredith had insisted on being near the toilets.

BANG. A door slammed somewhere in the depths of the museum. We all screamed; Mr Meredith shushed us. We had to remember, he said, there were caretakers looking after the building all night and, if we did hear any funny noises, that's who'd be making them. Not ghosts, dinosaurs or anything else that didn't exist any more and, come to that, it was probably time to go to sleep. As he said it, the City Hall clock struck eleven. I counted the chimes under my breath.

Carly tapped me on the shoulder as we were settling down but I ignored her, pretending to go to sleep straight away. I didn't. I kept my eyes open, fixed on the staircase I could just make out, a long, long way across the cold marble floor and now at eye level. Everyone fell eerily silent almost at once. There was just the sound of breathing and shuffling. Once, Mr Meredith sneezed. I was determined to keep my eyes open all night; I was going to; I was.

Each time I realised my eyes had been shut for more than a second, I made a big effort to open them again. And again. And again, until finally I must have given up — or given in — and fallen asleep.

When I woke sometime later, the City Hall clock was on its last chime again so I couldn't count how many chimes there'd been but, if anything, the room seemed even darker, the air even colder.

I could feel the hard marble beneath my sleeping bag and, as I wriggled around, trying to get comfier, I noticed that Carly's was empty. At the same moment, I spotted a shadow disappearing into the dark and I couldn't help but hear noisy feet clattering across the marble. Amazingly, the noise hadn't woken any of the others up. Where on earth did Carly think she was going? I found my torch and switched it on.

'Carly,' I whispered as loud as I dared. 'Come back!'

It was ridiculous. I should have just left her. Or I should have woken Mr Meredith. But for some strange reason Carly was standing, or rather crouching, at the bottom of the staircase – I could just make her out. Was she sleepwalking?

Without stopping to think, I wriggled out of my sleeping bag. It was freezing cold but at least I had thick socks on. The beam of my torch only tunnelled a little way into the dark. I took a few slidy steps across the floor, then a few more, moving further and further away from my sleeping friends.

'You're creeping me out, all right? Well done,' I hissed. Carly was just messing about, like before. I half expected the torch under the chin again. If she did that, I was going to scream.

But suddenly she did something I really hadn't expected. She turned and ran up the stairs. Up the stairs! And she clattered as she ran. I turned too, and skidded back across the Great Hall. It was ridiculous. Where did she think she was going? I could hear her on the landing on the first floor.

'Right, that's it,' I said. 'I'm going back to the others.'

I turned and screamed – just quickly, once – because there was Carly, shining her torch straight into my face. She covered my mouth with her hand. 'You're going to wake everyone up.'

'I thought that was you upstairs,' I whispered.

'Went to the loo,' she whispered back. 'Who's upstairs?'

That was a good question. We both looked up, slowly. Someone was up there, and that someone was trying to stifle a laugh.

Before I could stop her, Carly started climbing the stairs. 'Come back!' I hissed.

She did but only to take my hand and drag me up after her. 'It's one of the others,' she giggled. 'It's got to be.'

'No, it's not,' I whispered.

But she had hold of me and, against my will, I found myself walking up those cold stone steps, shaking with fear.

We were actually up on the first landing and I thought, just for a moment, I caught sight of a face peeping round the corner. A small face, pale as a winter moon.

'Hello?' said Carly.

The face disappeared.

'Let's go now,' I said but Carly was determined. 'It can't be a ghost,' she said. 'There's no such thing.'

Feet clattered across the marble landing, then one of the heavy upstairs gallery doors wheezed open and eased itself shut. My legs didn't feel as though they belonged to me any more as Carly pulled me round the corner and up the final flight of stairs.

'He's in here,' she said, pointing at the gallery.

'He?' I said.

'Yes, the little boy,' said Carly. 'He could be lost. Perhaps he got left behind when the museum closed.'

She didn't wait for my incredulous reply; she was already pushing the door open and shining her torch into the room but I followed her in, in spite of myself. I preferred to stick with her rather than make that long journey back downstairs on my own.

It was even darker in the gallery but suddenly there was a burst of laughter and a small child was peeping out at us from behind a pale, glowing statue. His face was almost as pale. Mask-like. Then he ran over to the other side of the room.

Holding my hand, Carly pulled me across the room and we were just getting close to his hiding place, another statue, when he shot past us again. I remembered this gallery: it was the one containing the famous French Impressionist paintings. The only one I didn't remember seeing before was one with a tall man and woman, their arms outstretched. As we ran past it, I couldn't help noticing how they looked as though they were calling to someone.

When did we realise that the little boy had gone? It was as though he had just vanished into thin air. I stood by the doors as Carly walked this way and that, looking for him. When she finally came up to me, I could see that her eyes were wide and she was breathing hard. Without saying a word, she dragged me through the doorway and suddenly we were running down the stairs as though our lives depended upon it.

'I thought I saw something,' she whispered as we clambered into our sleeping bags.

'What?' I asked. But she just pulled the sleeping bag over her head.

It was only the following morning, back up in the gallery, that I could take a guess at what Carly had seen. She still wouldn't say.

At least no one else noticed her shaking as I pulled her away from the strange painting I hadn't recognised, the one with the tall man and woman. *The Peasants* by Millet. Except their arms weren't outstretched anymore and they no longer seemed to be calling.

If you go and find the painting today, you'll see the man's hand resting protectively on the shoulder of a little boy. And, although he's hanging onto his mum and dad, he still looks as though he could burst out of the picture at any moment and do what all little boys want to do, just play.

Rhosyn's Grave

When I was ten years old, my Uncle Jac took me out with the Mari Lwyd men for the first and the last time. Why the first and last? Well, by the end of the night, we all swore that none of us would ever go again.

Have you heard of the Mari Lwyd? It was the custom to carry it from cottage to cottage, from farm to farm, on New Year's Eve, to bring good luck for the year to come. It was a real horse's skull, mounted on a pole, dressed up in a white sheet and bells and ribbons and stuff. I was scared stiff of it, I must admit, the way the skull's mouth with its two big teeth poked out of the front of the sheet. Ych!

Well, anyway, despite my fear of the Mari, I'd been on and on at Jac to take me with him. I suppose I felt I was missing out, stuck at home while they were all out celebrating. Finally, Jac said I could go as long as I was able to keep up. There were twelve of us but I was the only youngster. We had to walk for miles, carrying this thing, but Mam had wrapped me up in loads of sweaters and scarves to keep out the cold. Jac would take the odd nip of whisky which he reckoned did the same job.

So, anyway, we'd been to three or four farms and we were walking along this road, laughing and chatting, sometimes bursting into song. Each place we stopped at, the farmer's wife would offer us a drink – although nothing alcoholic for me, of course. Needless to say, Jac and his mates were in a very merry mood . . . but that was about to change.

It was a frosty night. The sky was milky with stars and the full moon, set in a creamy halo, poured down her light upon the road. The hedges glistened and the air smelt sharp and icy. A little way along, we came to a place where a track led off sharply to the left, then back on itself down a steep hill. I knew there was a cottage at the bottom of this track but I didn't know its name.

'Uncle Jac,' I said. 'Are we going to the cottage down there?'

The men all stopped and turned to look first at me and then at the track. '*Bedd Rhosyn?*' said Jac. 'I dunno. What do you think, boys?'

'There's new people down there now,' said one of the others. 'Just as well. It wasn't much good stood empty all those years.'

'Well, why not then?' chirped Jac. 'It's a way of welcoming the new folk, whoever they are.'

'You're right, Jac!'

So we left the road and started down the steep track and within a few yards we were deep in the shadows of some tall pine trees. It was hard to make out anything except the pale Mari trotting along in the darkness, bells jingling. Finally we made it down to the cottage, rapped the door and began singing our ancient song.

The door opened and there stood a man holding an oil lamp, and a woman cradling a sleepy little girl who peeped at us from the folds of her mother's shawl. We were invited in for a drink and spent a merry quarter of an hour hearing how Mr and Mrs Roberts were restoring the cottage and how they were going to change the name of it as soon as they could think of a better one. *Bedd Rhosyn*: Rhosyn's Grave. It wasn't a very cheerful name, was it? It wasn't even as if anyone could tell them who Rhosyn had been.

'Lovely folk,' Jac declared when we were back up on the road.

'Hey, we'd better get a move on, boys; it's nearly midnight and we're not even as far as Bryn yet!' said one of his mates, with a loud belch. So we set out again, trying to go a bit quicker, round the next bend and along another straight piece of road.

I heard it first, the drumming of a horse's hooves in the distance behind us. I called to Jac and he urged the rest of the merry men to keep to one side and let whoever it was pass. Trying not to tumble into the ditch, we all turned to look. The echoey sound of hooves drumming the ground carried on but they didn't seem to be getting any nearer. All the time we expected a horse and rider to come galloping round the bend but nothing appeared for a long while and we began to look questioningly at one another.

Then, all at once, there was a rush of wind and something shot past us like it had been fired from a cannon. After a moment's silence, there followed a deafening and unearthly hammering of hooves, which seemed to be racing to catch up, but in the same moment it was there, it was gone. No sign of a horse on the road ahead or any sound whatsoever. Bang – just like that! Gone.

'What was that?' someone whispered as we stared up the road.

'Mrs Roberts's ale is strong stuff, boys!' said another of the men and that sort of killed the tension. We started to laugh. Noises went funny at night, didn't they? They weren't the same as in the day. A loose horse had bolted and, in the morning, we'd have to check it wasn't one of ours. We began walking again and the only sounds that could be heard were the tramping of our feet and the soft jingling of bells.

But it wasn't long before the echoey drumming started again, ahead of us now. Someone whispered, 'It's coming back,' and we all stopped. The unmistakable sound of a horse's galloping hooves sounded a way down the road but again, nothing appeared for a long, long time. I felt Jac slip his arm through mine and pull me toward him. With my face buried in the front of his jacket, I heard his breath quicken. Then: 'Look out, boys!' he called, pulling me off the road as the same ear-splitting noise hammered past us and vanished as suddenly into the midnight air.

There was instant panic. Now we were certain that the horse was not of this world, that it had probably come straight from the Devil and, what's more, that it would be back. Just to add to the confusion, the Mari was passed hastily from hand to hand, jingling as though it didn't want to be left out of the excitement. I could hear the rasping of Jac's breath and felt the roughness of his jacket against my cheek. Then he took my hand and we began running up the road with the rest of them.

'If we cut through the fields, we'll reach Cwm Cog first.'

'Thank the Lord for that. We'll all dive into yours, right, Jac?'

'Right you are. Let's get going!'

But none of us really believed we'd seen the last of the hell horse and now behind us came the sound of hooves trotting in a controlled and determined way. One of the men whimpered with fear. With the trotting following us at a steady pace, we ran faster which, for me, meant being half dragged by my uncle. A man in front turned around and I saw a look of utter horror fix itself upon his face. Uncle Jac must have turned too because I heard him yell at me in a high voice quite unlike his own: 'Don't look round, my boy. Keep running. Don't look round whatever you do!'

I have never, in all my life, felt as scared as I did in that moment. We ran so fast, I felt as though my heart was about to explode. We ran so hard, I could hardly get one breath out before taking another and, all the time, Jac was urging me in that strange, strangled voice not to look round, not to look at whatever it was behind us. I didn't look. I didn't dare. I just kept running.

The gate was open, thank goodness, and we tumbled through it and down the field and didn't stop until we had reached the farmhouse. One of the men fiddled uselessly with the latch but then the whole lot of us pushing against the door sent it smashing to the ground. Not only the door but the door-frame too! We landed in a sweating, panicking pile right in the middle of the back kitchen where the rest of my family had gathered around the fire.

What had been following us? What nameless horror had chased us down the road? Mam made us all hot sweet tea which we took gratefully with shaking hands. For a while, Jac and the others kept quiet about what they had seen with me there listening but they were so on edge, it soon came tumbling out.

What they'd seen was a horse without a head.

A headless horse!

Over by the fireside, my great-grandfather shook his head. 'Why in the name of heaven did you go there?' he demanded. '*Bedd Rhosyn*? Why did you go there? In my day we never ventured near there, not with the Mari!'

'Why?' asked Jac.

'*Bedd Rhosyn*'s where Rhosyn is buried. Don't you know the story? Rhosyn was the favourite mare of the old boy who lived in the cottage, way before my time even. She died and he was heartbroken. But after she was buried some local lads dug her up and removed the skull. Turned it into the Mari Lwyd, didn't they? Poor old Harry never recovered from the shock. It turned him a bit funny.'

'Where's the Mari now?' asked Jac.

'I dropped it,' said one of his mates. 'I dropped it on the road and if you think I'm going back for it tonight . . .'

'There's no point,' said my great-grandfather. 'And you won't find it in the morning, either. Rhosyn came back for her head tonight, once you showed her where it was. Perhaps now at last she'll rest in peace.'

And he was right. No one ever saw Rhosyn again and the next morning the skull of the Mari was gone.

All we found, left lying on the road, was a white sheet . . . and a few ribbons . . . and bells.

A Witch in the Tree

There's a witch in the tree,
There's a witch in the tree.
If I run fast enough
Then she won't catch me!

For as long as anyone could remember, there'd been a witch in the oak tree by the infant playground. For years the little ones insisted they could see her up in the branches and it always seemed to happen on windy days. The teachers on duty tut-tutted into their mugs of coffee and told the older children off for trying to frighten the younger ones. It didn't do any good. The witch in the tree was an unshakable part of school folklore.

But though the story was unshakable, the tree itself wasn't, and one night, during a particularly nasty storm, it fell down. The next morning, open-mouthed infants gathered round the fallen tree with its exposed earthy roots.

To everyone's surprise the tree had a hollow heart, a rotten core around which it had continued growing; you could see it between where the tree's two biggest branches forked. The hollow was easily big enough for someone to crawl inside so the caretaker roped the tree off and the children were warned to stay away from it until the men came to remove it. The little ones did stay away, but they still couldn't keep their eyes off the tree where it lay like a stricken giant. Every single playtime that week, they stood in a line at the edge of the playground, munching snacks and watching the tree – like it was going anywhere. And, of course, there was endless speculation about what had happened to the witch. Had she made another home for herself on the roof of the school? Maybe the tree squashed her flat when it fell.

At the end of Friday's whole-school assembly, Mr Rhys, the headteacher, announced his brilliant idea. As wood carving happened to be his favourite hobby, he would take the best bits of the tree home and carve an Eisteddfod chair for the school. Everyone agreed that this was a wonderful plan, particularly since Mr Rhys was due to retire at the end of the year. It guaranteed that neither he nor the tree would ever be forgotten.

So the choicest parts of the tree's enormous trunk were cut into thick planks and delivered to Mr Rhys's home, where they were carried quickly through the house and down to his cellar workroom, before his wife, Gwen, could complain about sawdust being trodden into her carpets.

Despite its lack of windows, the cellar was bright and orderly with spotlights directed at the workbench and racks of chisels, fretsaws and planes. Henry Rhys loved spending time down there by himself, carving wood and listening to the radio.

He took to his latest project with enthusiasm. There was no rush to begin, which was good as it was the biggest challenge he'd ever tackled. As long as the chair was ready for St David's Day, all would be well. He spent hours handling the wood, taking notice of the way the grain ran, fingering the knots and wondering how to incorporate them into an overall design. The chair had to be eye-catching and unique, worthy of all the years Mr Rhys had devoted to the school. After days of struggle, making sketches of dragons and leeks, he suddenly struck upon an idea which was so brilliantly obvious he was amazed he hadn't thought of it in the first place. A tree! Henry would carve a chair shaped like a tree. The legs could be the roots, the branches would interlace like Celtic knotwork and the oak leaves and acorns would crown the winning bard. Splendid!

The first sign that something was wrong occurred about a month later. Each evening after tea, Henry would head down to his workroom, rarely emerging before midnight, and the same thing at weekends. But one Thursday evening there was a phone call, something to do with school, which his wife thought important enough to bother him about. 'Henry, phone!' she called from the top of the cellar steps.

There was no answer but he probably hadn't heard with the radio on so she began to descend the steps. The back of the Eisteddfod chair was facing her and she could tell that Henry was sitting in it. She could see his head and shoulders through holes in the back of the chair.

'Henry, phone!' she repeated. To her surprise, he didn't move. His hand remained absolutely motionless on the arm of the chair. Gwen walked around him very slowly. She reached over and switched off the radio.

'Henry?' she said, suddenly afraid. He was just sitting there, staring into space, his eyes glazed over. He was breathing heavily, making a low rasping sound, and beads of perspiration stood out on his forehead. She put her hand on his arm and shook it. 'Henry?'

He blinked and a shudder ran through his entire body as he turned to face his wife. 'I must have dropped off,' he said, slowly.

'It looked like you were having a funny turn.'

'I'm fine,' he said. 'I must have been dreaming.' He wiped his hand over his brow and stared at his sweaty palm. 'It was so strange. I was in this place, a place I seemed to know. I recognised it but I couldn't quite remember where it was. It was the strangest feeling.'

Gwen scolded him for overdoing it, grafting away for hours each evening after a full day at school. He agreed to go to bed early but not before showing her how far he'd got with the chair. It was the first time she'd seen it and although she never normally took an interest in her husband's hobby, she couldn't help but admire what he'd done. Although still very rough, the tree was clearly visible and she thought the way the branches weaved in and out of each other was very clever. If you stared for long enough, you could almost convince yourself that those branches were moving.

Despite his wife's protests, Henry was soon back at his carving, working harder than ever. Every single evening, although he'd start by promising himself that he was definitely not going to sit down upon the chair, a dreadful weariness made it impossible for him to do anything else. Then he'd wake up to find himself sitting bolt upright, sweating heavily, with the same uncanny feeling that he'd been somewhere he knew very, very well.

The staff and pupils at school soon noticed the difference in Henry Rhys. He had always been a calm, friendly, encouraging sort of headmaster but he just seemed to change overnight. From the start of the spring term he seldom emerged from his office and, when he did, it was always with a scowl on his face. He was grumpy with everyone, staff and pupils alike. Unbelievably, considering how well loved he had always been, the teachers began talking as though they couldn't wait for Mr Rhys to retire.

'I heard him snapping at someone on the phone again this morning ...'

'Only a few months to go, thank goodness ...'

'You know what's weird? All he does in his room is stand and stare out of the window. Stares across at the infant yard with this blank look on his face. I see him all the time when I'm out on duty ...'

To everyone's relief, once the chair was finished, Henry Rhys's mood lightened a lot and by the time St David's Day arrived, he seemed quite back to his old self. Everyone at school was dying to see the new Eisteddfod chair but they had to wait for it to be unveiled.

It stood at the back of the stage, draped in a red velvet cloth while children performed their Eisteddfod pieces, but then the great moment came and it was carried to the front. Mr Rhys chose two reception children to unveil the chair and as they did so, everyone in the hall gasped. There was a moment's silence followed by torrents of applause which went on and on and on. Mr Rhys's chair was a work of art. There was so much movement about the way it had been carved and the detail of the knotty roots and intricately twisting branches was breathtaking, to say nothing of the multitude of delicate leaves and acorns. Eventually everyone calmed down and the Deputy Head stood up to thank Mr Rhys for the terrific effort he had put into making the chair. Then she wondered who would be lucky enough to be the first to sit in it.

An excited murmur travelled around the hall as the time had come to announce the Bard. The winning poem on the theme of 'Nature's Playground' was read out and then the pen-name of the winning poet. Everyone clapped and cheered when 'Stardust' stood up and they could see that it was Elinor Evans from Year Six. Once the robe had been placed about her shoulders, she was escorted down the middle of the hall. As he did every year, Mr Rhys asked the children, 'A oes heddwch? Is there peace?' and after their third reply, he gestured for Elinor to sit upon the Eisteddfod chair.

Everybody in the hall saw at once that something was wrong.

Only later did they see it from Elinor's viewpoint, when she tried her best to explain how it felt: 'All the faces in the hall seemed to dissolve before my eyes and the voices around me dwindled to nothing. Instead, I heard the sound of a great rushing wind and, as the swirling mists gradually cleared, I realised I was in a different place entirely but one I felt I must know very well. I was sitting high up in the air, looking down at lots of little children running around in circles, chanting:

> There's a witch in the tree,
> There's a witch in the tree.
> If I run fast enough
> Then she won't catch me!

The next moment I was on the floor and someone was patting my face, and voices were calling my name. As they carried me away, I was surprised to see that the chair was lying all around me in pieces as though it had been ripped apart.'

So what had happened? Even those who had witnessed it were at a loss to explain.

How could you account for the fact that the moment Elinor sat in the Eisteddfod chair, its branches started to move and twist around her arms and chest and in the same way its roots began imprisoning her legs? How could it have taken the strength of Mr Rhys and six other desperate teachers to prise the chair away from her, hacking at the roots and branches before it could swallow her up entirely?

A shocked Henry Rhys helped the caretaker make a bonfire of what was left of the chair on the school field that very afternoon, once all the children had been sent safely home to recover from the ordeal. The grown-ups made doubly sure that every last splinter of wood was hoovered up from the stage.

And as they watched the thick smoke billowing from the fire out on the field, the howl of the wind which bore it away sounded for all the world like the cry of an angry witch.

Smileys

There was a tap on the window behind me but I carried on playing my game, pretending I hadn't heard. Tap, tap, tap. I gritted my teeth. Tap, tap, tap! I sprang round.

'You'll break that window!' I shouted.

Dad beamed, pointed over his shoulder and made flapping movements with his hands.

'Cetti's warbler!' he cried, nodding excitedly and, as he did so, rain tumbled off the peak of his hood and down his nose. But he'd spotted a Cetti's warbler: what did he care? 'Thought it was a reed warbler but no. Very rare in this part of Wales.' He looked like he'd won the Lottery.

I remembered what Mum had said: when it gets too boring, just ring and I'll come and get you. Not 'if' but 'when', that's how she'd put it, and Mum always chose her words carefully. It was now Monday, day three of our week at the cottage, but although my hand had hovered several times over my mobile I hadn't actually given in and rung. Yet.

'I'm fine here, thanks, Dad.' I waved lamely. He waved back, looking a little disappointed, then he turned and went off down the garden path. For some reason, I rose from my chair and walked to the window. Light drizzle had been falling since first light but it was now raining good and proper. I watched as Dad paced down the road a little way before turning off into the marshes. Who else but Dad would rent a holiday cottage at the edge of marshes, miles from anywhere? Even the beach was so far in the distance you could barely see it. I knew what he'd had in mind, the two of us with our flasks and sandwiches, off birdwatching every day and in all weathers. It wasn't my idea of fun. I found it impossible to get worked up about great crested whassnames and lesser spotted doo-dahs, no matter how rare.

As my breath hit the cold glass, something appeared. It was a smiley face, like you'd attach to an email or draw on your pencil case, or somewhere like that. Not a true smiley, on account of the fact it wasn't smiling. Its mouth was just a straight line across. There must have been condensation on the window at some time and someone had drawn on it. If they're not rubbed out, these drawings keep popping up each time the window mists. I breathed a bit more on the face, which became clearer, then I noticed a 'B' next to it. I breathed heavily all across the glass to reveal a word.

BORING.

I couldn't help chuckling to myself, imagining some kid standing where I was standing, staring out at the pouring rain and the marshes with nothing more interesting to do than doodle on the window. Perhaps his parent was a birdwatching nut, too.

That evening we had beans on toast – again. After that I played my game while Dad scrutinised his bird manual. He was trying desperately to get me interested in the Cetti's warbler's eggs and how they compared with the eggs of every other warbler on earth.

'Dad!' I snapped. 'I'm not interested, OK? I couldn't care less about birdwatching.'

Dad took off his reading glasses. 'Shall we do something different tomorrow then?'

'I don't care.'

He went to fill the kettle. 'One of those leaflets said something about a local museum,' he said cheerily over his shoulder.

Great, I thought, a twelve-mile journey to see a bucket from 1851.

'It's all right, Dad. I'd rather not.'

'I expect you'll be off somewhere else with your mum and Vince before school starts.' Dad flicked the kettle on.

'Nah,' I said. 'We went skiing at Easter, remember?'

'I bet that was fun.' Dad turned around and smiled at me.

'It was brilliant,' I said without looking up from my game.

Dad forgot to make the tea. When the water boiled, he was out of the room and there was something wrong with the stupid kettle; it wouldn't switch itself off. Clouds of steam filled the room, turning it into a sauna. Sighing, I dragged myself from the table and switched it off. I noticed that there was another smiley drawn on the window behind the sink, like the one in the living room except this one had raised eyebrows. Next to it was a question: STILL BORED? Wow. Someone really had had a great holiday.

The next morning as Dad prepared breakfast, I sat on the bed, my finger resting on the 'send' button, wondering if I should send my text or not.

mum im bored can u come 4 me 2moro pls? can u think of gd excuse? dont want dad 2 b sad. Dxxxx!

Somehow I just couldn't press it. The problem was I only ever saw Dad for odd weeks here and there since Mum married Vince and we went to live the other end of the country. I missed him, but then when we did see each other, it usually ended up like this. He was either catching up frantically on paperwork or tramping round the countryside with binoculars and flask, totally wrapped up in his hobby.

My eyes travelled round the room while I debated what to do. They suddenly halted at the window. My bedroom was in the roof space so the small window was quite low to the floor. There was another smiley. Another one. Except this was a frowning smiley. It was strange because I could have sworn the window had been clear earlier. I went and knelt beside it, wondering if there was another hidden message to discover. Had the phantom bored holidaymaker struck again? I breathed all over the glass and a message appeared.

DON'T SEND IT.

Startled, I scuttled back as far as the bed. Don't send it? Don't send what? The text? A shiver ran right through me and I continued staring at the message as though I still couldn't have read it properly. How could that smiley be telling me what to do? It just wasn't possible.

'Breakfast!' Dad called up the stairs.

I picked up the mobile, switched it off and put it back on the bedside cabinet. I hadn't sent the text but it was saved so perhaps I would later. Before going down to breakfast, I crouched at arm's length from the window and rubbed out what was on there with my dressing-gown sleeve.

But of course it was completely ridiculous, an absurd coincidence and, as I sat in the kitchen after breakfast, I came up with several different reasons why that particular message had been written on the window. Some bored kids might have written a funny postcard and hesitated to send it. Perhaps they were just messing about with their own mobile phone. One thing was for sure: if I wasn't so bored myself, that message would not have given me the fright it had, which only added weight to the argument for cutting the holiday short.

Dad came into the living room dressed for the great drizzly outdoors, binoculars at the ready. 'Well, if you're certain you don't want to do anything together today ...' he began.

I picked up my game. 'That's right,' I said.

'You'll be bored sitting here all alone,' he said.

'I've been bored since coming here!' I made an *isn't that obvious?* face without even raising my head.

'OK,' said Dad. 'Any problems, I'm just over there. Shout from the window if you need anything.'

'OK,' I said.

'I'll be back in fifteen minutes to see you're all right.'

'No need.'

Off he went. I knew I was being mean but I just

couldn't help it: I was so, so, so, so bored. Nothing Dad could suggest was remotely appealing. The one time we'd driven over to the beach, I just stood around freezing while he spent a whole hour comparing herring-gull wingspans. But it made me feel rotten to be so mean. Perhaps it really was better all round if I made that call to Mum. Perhaps, deep down, Dad would be happier too if I left. Then he could roam about the marshes to his heart's content rather than having to stay so close to the cottage all the time.

At that moment I froze again – as I caught sight of a brand-new smiley on the window above the kitchen sink. The kettle had boiled recently and this was another frowning smiley, yet different from the one in the bedroom. It was frowning harder, its eyebrows deep and menacing. I sat staring at it for a little while then, on autopilot, stood up and reached over to turn the kettle on again. The water came quickly to the boil, pumping out clouds of steam. After a few moments, I flicked the switch off and the clouds cleared to reveal a new, horrible message on the glass:

SOMETHING'S COMING.

My legs gave way and the chair caught me. Surely Dad wouldn't be doing this? He didn't have a sick sense of humour. But the next moment I noticed that every single shiny surface in that kitchen, from the kettle itself to the door of the microwave, was now carrying the same message.

SOMETHING'S COMING. SOMETHING'S COMING. SOMETHING'S COMING.

I ran out of the room, only to be confronted by the hall mirror:

SOMETHING'S COMING.

I tore round the corner and there it was, scrawled all over the telly screen:

SOMETHING'S COMING.

I was breathing so hard, I wondered if I'd have enough breath to scream. I rattled the catch to try and open the window. It instantly steamed up to reveal a final, horrifying message:

HERE IT IS!

I released the catch and opened the window, tried to scream but nothing came out. I could see Dad sitting on his little stool a stone's throw from the garden wall, his back towards me, peering through his binoculars. And there, approaching from his left, something was moving, slowly, through the reeds, flattening them as it came. My stomach churns when I think of that vile-looking thing, which was like no animal I recognised. I literally shuddered to look at it. I couldn't see its face but I'll never forget the way it seemed to pant with excitement, its ribcage moving in and out, visible beneath the damp, straggly fur. All the time it was creeping up on Dad, getting closer and closer, and I wanted to shout and scream to warn him but I simply couldn't, like I was in the middle of a nightmare. Or like I'd been hypnotised.

45

The spell broke. I had to do something. I raced to the front door and grabbed a walking stick from the coat stand, fumbling to get the door open. I flew down the path and down the road. Dad rose and turned to face me so he still wasn't aware of what was creeping up on him. I ran onto the marsh, my knees buckling as I stumbled over the hummocky ground straight towards Dad, shouting at him to get out of the way. As he saw the stick raised above my head, his quizzical expression turned to one of panic. He dodged as I struck at the large shadow into which the creature was already dissolving. It snarled at me as I swiped and swiped at it with my stick, and I glimpsed a pair of wicked, all-too-human eyes which melted into the air last of all. I don't know why, but when it was gone, I was certain in my heart that it was never coming back. I was so glad, I began to cry. I dropped the walking stick and rain trickled down my face, mingling with tears as Dad put his arms round me, holding me safe and kissing the top of my head.

It seems strange now, but at the time it felt right not to talk about what had happened then or for the rest of the holiday. Because I didn't phone or text Mum; I stayed. And even though birdwatching still wouldn't feature on my top ten list of things to do, I did start spending more time with Dad. By the Friday, I could almost tell the difference between a Cetti's warbler and a reed warbler. We also took a couple of trips to different places and it felt really good to be together, not at all the way it had been.

So when on Friday morning, the final morning, a smiley appeared on my bedroom window – a proper smiling smiley, no message – I smiled back at it briefly before rubbing it out hastily with my sleeve.

Trust

———

'It's all about trust,' said Iwan. 'Just let yourself fall and we'll catch you.'

Nadine gulped and, as instructed, let herself fall, keeping her legs straight. As promised, many hands caught her and she was pushed gently from hand to hand round in a circle. She couldn't help but giggle: it almost felt ticklish and, after the first few uneasy seconds, it really was easy to trust, to let yourself go, knowing no one was going to drop you.

When it was time to take off the blindfold, she beamed at the other kids standing around her. 'It's easy,' she said. 'Try it. It's fun!'

Nadine was pleased she'd had the first go. Iwan, the writer and director, was sure to have spotted her nerve and she was determined to do well in the audition. Her goal, of course, was to win the star part of Princess Gaia. Looks-wise she was there already, with her long blonde hair; and she was taller than any of the other girls. The musical was set in another galaxy and she reckoned she'd look better in a lycra spacesuit than any of them. And she knew she could sing.

A few of the other kids seemed to know one another from different drama groups but Nadine didn't know a soul. It was better that way. She felt braver because she'd come alone.

'Let's take five,' said Iwan, once a couple more kids had tried the trust exercise. Several had refused to do it.

'Idiots!' Nadine thought to herself. They all sat in a big circle on the stage and Mari, Iwan's sidekick, handed out bottles of water.

'So, how do you feel about acting in a real Victorian theatre?' said Iwan. 'You know, the Royal's one of the best-preserved old theatres this side of the Severn Bridge?'

'It's quite . . . small, isn't it?' said a boy named Benedict.

'By our standards today,' said Iwan. 'But there's something about these old theatres, don't you think?'

'I think it has an amazing atmosphere,' said Nadine, flashing her brightest smile. A girl named Martha, who Nadine already had marked down as her biggest rival, rolled her eyes. Nadine wasn't exaggerating, though. Somehow the fact that the theatre was small made it more impressive. The balconies seemed to be teetering, on the brink of tumbling down upon the stage and the boxes were so close you could almost touch them. Imagine all that rich dark-red and gold lit up by flickering gaslight in Victorian times. What would it be like to star in a play in this theatre? Nadine couldn't wait to find out.

'So are there any ghosts?' asked Benedict. A shivery snigger went round the group. 'I mean to say, there's always a ghost in an old theatre, isn't there?'

Iwan gazed around with a whisper of a smile. There was a second wave of laughter as he wiggled his eyebrows up and down. 'Yes,' he said seriously at last. 'There is a ghost but it's a sad story. She was a young actress who died here. Actually she's supposed to have fallen to her death.' The sniggering stopped and several pairs of eyes drifted up to the highest balcony.

'From up there?' asked Benedict.

Iwan shook his head. 'No one ever sees her but they . . . sense her presence sometimes. One or two people have said they've felt her touch them.'

Martha shrieked and leapt to her feet but it was just Robbie tapping her arm, messing about. Everyone burst out laughing except Martha, who stared daggers at Robbie.

'Enough ghost stories,' cried Iwan, springing to his feet. 'I feel we need to do a few more warm-ups before the auditions. And because some of you refused to do the last trust exercise . . . I think we should do another!'

There were several groans.

'I'm up for that!' said Nadine.

This time Iwan put them in pairs and they had to take it in turns to wear a blindfold while their partner led them around the stage, first by two hands, then one hand, then one finger. Iwan moved them upstage. They were all going to do this exercise together but Iwan assured them that he was watching and no way was anyone in danger of plunging into the orchestra pit.

Nadine wasn't best pleased to find herself partnering Martha but the two girls managed to exchange the briefest of smiles before Nadine agreed to put on the blindfold first. Martha's hands were small and cool and Nadine followed as they led her in and out of the other couples. Martha actually did a good job of making sure they didn't collide with anyone and by the time Nadine was following Martha's fingertip, she was totally trusting of her rival.

When they swapped, Nadine made a big effort to do the leading job just as well, even though she was also conscious of Iwan, willing him to look more at her than anyone else.

Everyone had been sent a short scene from *Gaia Returns* to learn for the audition. It was the scene where Princess Gaia first meets evil General Jaxx so you either learnt the boy's or the girl's part. Nadine swallowed nervously when she found out they'd all be watching one another perform the scene. She had to work hard to act as though she didn't mind. When her turn came, she was partnered with Robbie, who turned out to be quite good even though he messed up a couple of lines. Again, after the first few nervous seconds, Nadine felt quite confident acting in front of the group. She knew she could trust herself completely. She was even pleased when Robbie messed up because she was the one who managed to smooth over the mistakes – which made her look even better. She even loved the feeling that Martha's eyes were boring into her and willing her to fail. Nadine wasn't going to fail, of that she was certain.

At lunchtime, Mari handed out sandwiches, fruit and bottles of water, and all the kids sat around the stage in twos or threes. Nadine didn't mind that she was alone; it gave her an excuse to sit near the director.

'Do you mind if I sit here?' she asked Iwan and Mari. 'I don't really know anyone.'

Then she dried up. She couldn't think of anything else to say and the three of them sat in silence for a while. Of the hundreds of questions Nadine could have asked about the play, she suddenly couldn't think of any. Instead, she said, 'Can't you tell us any more about the ghost?'

'Oh, the ghost,' said Iwan. 'What do you want to know?'

'Who was she?' By the smirk on Iwan's face, Nadine was afraid she had asked something stupid.

'Her name's Lizzie. She was a young actress, probably about your age. She was an understudy. That's someone who'll stand in if one of the actors can't go on for some reason. Well, the night Lizzie died, the lead actress was taken ill and Lizzie was going to replace her. You can imagine how excited she felt but there was an accident and . . . she fell. That's the story.'

'Do you believe it?' asked Nadine.

'No,' said Iwan. 'Like someone said, every old theatre seems to have a ghost. I'm not a believer myself.'

'But what was she doing up there?' Benedict had wandered over and was looking up at the balcony again.

'I didn't say she fell from up there,' replied Iwan.

'From where then?'

But Iwan was already on his feet, clapping his hands and telling everyone it was time to get back to work.

The afternoon was a singing test. They'd all been sent a song to learn and Nadine had been practising it for weeks. She was glad the rest of the group had to remain backstage for this part of the audition, but when her turn arrived and she had to step out onto the stage on her own, she felt very exposed. Nadine was fully lit but the rest of the auditorium was in darkness and, as she shaded her eyes, she could just make out Iwan and Mari sitting in the middle of the third row.

'OK, Nadine,' called Iwan. 'Are you ready to sing for us?'

'As I'll ever be!' Nadine called back, pleased she could still make a joke.

Music began to play and Nadine launched into the song. She did her best to inject emotion into it and managed to hit the high note at the end of the chorus. Again, after the first few seconds, she knew she could trust herself to give a good performance.

Suddenly all the lights went out and the music shut off. Nadine was standing alone in the pitch black.

'Oh, great,' she heard Iwan say. Then he called, 'Must be a power failure. Nadine, stay exactly where you are. I'll have to try and get out of here and find the manager. Stay where you are, OK?'

'All right,' she heard herself say. But as she stood there in total darkness, a horrible feeling began creeping over her. 'Mari?' she called.

'It's OK; I'm still here,' said Mari. 'They won't be long; don't worry.'

Minutes passed which felt like hours. Every so often, Mari would say something to let her know she was still there.

'It's taking ages,' said Nadine.

'Knowing Iwan, he's probably popped into the bar on the way back . . . Joke!' Mari added quickly.

More minutes passed. Then Nadine felt a hand on her arm, which made her jump but before she could say anything, the hand had slid its way down her arm and had slipped itself into her own hand. At that moment, the music started up again, filling the stage much louder than before but it wasn't accompanied by any lights. The hand felt small and cool. Was it Martha's hand, or Mari's? But Martha was backstage, wasn't she?

'Which of you is it?' said Nadine, but it was impossible to hear the reply because the music was so loud.

The fingers of the hand stroked Nadine's comfortingly and then began to pull her gently, urging her to follow. It was so strangely like the trust exercise from earlier that Nadine half expected to be led around and about all over the stage. But the hand was only pulling in one direction and Nadine guessed that it was Mari who had come to fetch her. She just had to trust that Mari knew where she was going in the dark.

At last, the song came to an end and the music stopped. 'Are you all right?' called Mari.

But that wasn't right. Mari's voice was still down in the third row but her hand was on stage holding Nadine's.

'Who's holding my hand?' Nadine had suddenly turned very cold. The only response to her question was a tightening of the hand's grip and a more urgent pull.

'Get off!' she yelled, trying to release herself. But there was an iron strength about that little hand and its owner seemed determined she should continue to follow. Nadine screamed and pulled backwards and she could hear Mari shouting her name helplessly below.

Another hand grabbed hold of Nadine's other arm

and pulled her. She dropped to the floor, crying with fright, but the hands kept pulling and pulling her and in spite of herself, she continued to slide steadily across the stage.

At last the lights snapped on.

'Stay exactly where you are!'

Nadine was blinded by brightness and the blur of her tears but she could hear footsteps racing through the auditorium and up onto the stage. It was Iwan who yanked her away from the edge of the hole that had opened up in front of her. A trapdoor had fallen open, revealing a long drop into darkness.

'Someone was pulling me towards it,' cried Nadine. 'Someone wanted me to fall down there.'

Iwan was pale with shock. 'It couldn't be,' he whispered.

'What do you mean?' Mari had her arms round Nadine now, and Nadine was sobbing uncontrollably.

Iwan turned to Mari. 'Lizzie. The story is she's jealous of the more talented young actresses,' he whispered. 'I've never believed it. But that's exactly how she's supposed to have died, during her one and only performance. She fell through that trapdoor and broke her neck.'

The Ghost Zoner

Glyn was always showing off some geeky new gadget he'd built. His bedroom was full of bits of computers and instruction manuals. Hardly anything he made ever worked properly, though, so I wasn't convinced the first time he showed me the 'ghost zoner'.

'What's it do? Tell you if there's ghosts about?' I rotated the metal box in my hands. It was the size of a cornflake packet with a compass stuck in its middle, together with a thermometer, various dials and switches and, sticking out of the front, what looked suspiciously like a sawn-off egg whisk.

'Not exactly,' Glyn replied. 'It doesn't tell you if there's a ghost, just if conditions are right for a ghost to be there.'

'You've got to be joking!' I laughed, handing him back the daft-looking contraption.

'Look, I found it in one of Dad's magazines from when he was a kid. See what it says.' Glyn handed me a battered copy of something called *Wonder Gadgets*. On the second page, a kid was fiddling with the switches on a similar-looking machine while the picture opposite showed a wobbly white ghoul hovering in mid air. I began reading the article aloud.

BE THE ENVY OF YOUR FRIENDS – BUILD YOUR OWN AMAZING GHOST ZONER!

Imagine having the power to detect paranormal zones – the places where ghosts just love to hang out! All you need is a box, an egg whisk (I knew it!) and bits and pieces that can easily be found in your dad's shed . . .

'And you wasted how much time putting it together?' I asked.

'I'd only have wasted my time if it didn't work.' Glyn looked smug.

'You're saying it works?'

'Yes, it does!' His voice dropped to a whisper. 'First time I used it, I found a ghost zone. You'll never guess where?'

'Surprise me.'

'Right in the middle of the shopping centre. Imagine: all those shoppers walking around, completely unaware that there's a paranormal zone right under their noses. I knew you'd be surprised.'

It's true my jaw had hit the floor, but not with the kind of surprise Glyn imagined. I was doing my best not to crease up laughing.

'Are you coming then? To the shopping centre?'

'Nah. Supposed to be going swimming,' I lied. There was no way I was being seen in public with Glyn's nutty-looking egg-whisk machine.

A couple of days later, he started on about it again as we walked home from school.

'It's not surprising there's a ghost zone in the shopping centre,' he began. 'We had a lesson today on local history and we went online to find photos. Guess what? Back in the old days, there was a crossroads right in the middle. And there was a gibbet there. That's where they used to hang people. Robbers and murderers and highwaymen.'

'You're making it up,' I said.

'No, I swear! I found an old image of the crossroads. The gibbet wasn't in the photo but it said underneath that it had stood there for hundreds of years. One of the roads was even called Gib Lane.'

'But how do you know your ghost zone's in that exact same place?'

'It must be. It's too much of a coincidence. Come with me and I'll show you,' Glyn said.

'You haven't brought the ghost zoner with you?' I asked.

He patted his rucksack with pride. It looked like I would have to be seen in public with the crazy machine after all.

The shops weren't that busy and a few of them like the butcher's and baker's were already closed. Glyn took off his rucksack and wrestled out the ghost zoner, taking care not to snap off the twanging whisk. He held the machine against his stomach and flicked a switch. A low buzzing sound began.

'If this is a wind-up, I'm going to kill you,' I said through gritted teeth. I'd already spotted a couple of girls nudging each other and laughing as they went past.

'Just watch what happens,' said Glyn. We walked slowly forward until we arrived at the very centre, a square paved area cut off at each corner by raised-brick flower beds and benches. All of a sudden, the buzzing turned into a high-pitched whistle and the pin on the compass began spinning wildly this way and that.

'Look at the thermometer,' he said. The mercury was dropping faster than you would believe.

'That's really weird,' I said. I passed my hand in front

of the whisk but it made no difference. The machine carried on whistling and the compass continued to spin.

'Electromagnetic activity,' said Glyn. 'It happens every single time I come here. And I've noticed something else. Hardly any shoppers walk through this bit if they can help it. Nine out of ten people will walk the long way round and I bet they don't even realise they're doing it. Something's telling them to stay away. This is definitely a place where paranormal things could happen.'

'So what about him? He's decided to stay here.' I pointed to the man on the wall, the living statue who was standing on the edge of one of the raised-brick flower beds.

'I dunno,' said Glyn.

From time to time these living statues appear in the shopping centre, usually on a Saturday. My favourite used to be a man in an old-fashioned frock coat and top hat who was completely blue from head to foot. If you gave him ten pence he would lift his hat or shake hands with you, then freeze in a new position and stay there for ages, not even blinking. Crowds of people would gather round and give him money.

This new statue wasn't in the same league as the blue man. In fact, it was fair to say that this one hadn't made much of an effort at all. He was dressed in a long brown robe with a hood that draped down and hid his face completely. His hands were the only visible part of his body and they simply rested limply by his sides. They were big, rough-looking, man's hands.

'No one's taking any notice of him,' I said. 'Can you turn that thing off for a minute?'

The whistling was starting to get on my nerves. Glyn switched off the ghost zoner.

We looked at each other with the same thought in mind and went to sit on the bench opposite the living statue. I looked at my watch: it was four o'clock. Judging by the piddly number of copper coins on the pavement in front of the statue, he hadn't had a very successful day.

'This isn't the best place for him to do business,' said Glyn. 'Someone ought to tell him.'

'Go on then. You're the one with the evidence,' I said.

But neither of us did anything. We just continued to stare at the lifeless-looking statue. His shoulders were slumped forwards. His rough robes hung right down and covered his feet.

'Not exactly entertaining,' I said.

'Give him some money; he might do something,' said Glyn.

'I don't think I've got any,' I lied, fingering the coin in my coat pocket.

'Me neither.'

I carried on playing with the coin until I couldn't stand the suspense any longer. I plucked it out of my pocket and shook it in Glyn's face. 'All right. I suppose it's down to me as usual!' I sprang to my feet crossly. Glyn stuck out his lower lip and shrugged his shoulders. I walked a few paces towards the statue then hesitated and turned to look at my friend.

'Go on!' he mouthed.

I took three slow steps forward and tossed my ten pence down onto the pavement. Nothing happened so I coughed. The statue stood stock still, no handshake, no funny wave, no nothing. The hands remained hanging from the loose sleeves of the robe and moved not so much as a fingertip. I looked back at Glyn but he just shrugged his shoulders again.

'Aren't you going to do something?' I asked the statue.

There was no reply.

'No wonder you haven't collected much money,' I said.

He still didn't move. Who did this guy think he was?

'Well, if you don't want it . . . I'll just take my money back then,' I muttered. But leaning forward to pick up my ten pence, I couldn't tear my eyes away from the statue and as I bent lower, I finally saw his feet. They were dirty and they were bare but it was something else about them that made me catch my breath. *The feet weren't standing on the wall at all. They weren't standing on anything. They were dangling in space with their toes pointing downwards.*

In spite of myself, I glanced up under the hood. I

didn't want or need much of a look. The expression upon that face told me everything in a split second. The gibbet! Whoever he was, he'd ended his life hanging from the gibbet.

'RUN!' I shouted to Glyn, and we did, all the way up the street. We rounded the corner and came to a halt by the library.

'Wait,' panted Glyn. 'I've left the ghost zoner back on the bench.'

'No way am I going back there,' I panted, bent double with my hands on my knees. I was trembling all over. 'Tell you what though, Glyn, I'll take back what I said. It works. I'll give you that. Your ghost zoner really does work!'